Luna's Yum Yum Dim Sum

Natasha Yim

Illustrated by Violet Kim

Charlesbridge

It's Luna's birthday! Ma Ma and Ba Ba are taking Luna and her brothers to a dim sum restaurant for a special birthday lunch.

The restaurant is a noisy, busy place.
Voices chatter, chatter, buzz, buzz.
Chopsticks click, clickety, clack.

"Over here!"

Servers in white tunics push carts filled with plates and bamboo baskets of dim sum. Warm smells of dumplings, buns, and sweet desserts tickle Luna's nose.

"I'll take one!"

"What would you like?" asks Ba Ba.

"Pork buns!" cries Luna.

"Two baskets, please," says Kai, her big brother.

"We love pork buns!" says little brother Benji.

Ba Ba waves to the dim sum server.
He orders two baskets of char siu bao.

"Three pork buns in each basket," Luna says.

"Two for me, two for Kai, and two for Luna!" cries Benji.

Kai takes a pork bun.

Benji takes a pork bun.

"Yum yum, dim sum!" cries Luna. She grabs a pork bun . . .

Oh no!

Splat!

Luna takes another bun.

"That's all you get," says Kai.

"Two for me, two for Kai, and one for Luna!"
Benji exclaims.

"It's my birthday! I can't have just one!"
Luna wails.

"But there are only two buns left," says Kai.

"Who gets them?" asks Benji.

"The oldest gets another bun," declares Kai. "Ma Ma tells us to always respect our elders."

"And older kids should take care of younger kids," says Benji, "so I get another bun."

"But I'm the birthday girl!" Luna says.

Kai, Luna, and Benji glare at one another.

"It wouldn't be fair for one person to be left out," Luna says finally. "Let's cut each bun in half."

"Half for each of us," says Benji.
"Who gets the extra?"

"Well, the tallest person needs more food," says Kai.

"And the shortest person needs more food to grow taller," says Benji.

"But it's my birthday!" insists Luna.

"How about we cut the half in half?" says Kai.

"But that would be two pieces for three people. We'd be right back where we started!" exclaims Luna in dismay.

"I know," says Kai. "Let's go by the animals of the lunar calendar. I'm a rat. That's the first animal on the calendar, so I should get the extra."

"But I'm a dragon," says Benji, puffing his chest. "I'm bigger than a rat. I can stomp on a rat anytime."

"Tigers are the bravest," Luna says.

Kai, Luna, and Benji stare at the fluffy, delicious half bun.

"How about this?" Luna says. "Let's divide the half into three pieces."

"That's fair," says Benji.

Kai sighs. "But the pieces would be so small."

"**Wait!**" says Luna.

Yum yum, dim sum!

What Is Dim Sum?

Dim sum is a meal of bite-sized foods, traditionally served in bamboo baskets from push carts. In some modern restaurants, dim sum is ordered from a menu. But ordering from a cart is much more fun!

Dim sum originated in Southern China. It literally means "to touch the heart" in Cantonese, a dialect of Chinese. Dim sum is also sometimes called yum cha, which means "drink tea." In the old days, teahouses were built along trade routes to provide refreshment for weary travelers. Later, small snacks were added to go along with the tea. And dim sum was born!

The Chinese Zodiac

According to legend, the Jade Emperor once invited all the animals to participate in a big race. The first twelve animals to swim across the river would appear in the lunar calendar in the order in which they reached the other bank.

The rat won the race, so it is the first animal in the Chinese zodiac. After the rat came the ox, tiger, rabbit, dragon, snake, horse, goat, monkey, rooster, dog, and pig. Each animal has its own year in the zodiac cycle, and the cycle repeats every twelve years. In the story, Luna, Kai, and Benji compare their zodiac animals to see who should get the last piece of pork bun.

Exploring the Math

Luna and her two brothers plan to share six buns equally. But when one bun falls on the floor, they are left with only five to share. As they look for a fair solution, they cut buns in half and consider cutting a half into two or three parts. They recognize that half of a half is a small part and that a half divided into three yields even smaller parts.

As children find ways to divide up amounts fairly, they begin to make sense of division, fractions, and the notion of parts and wholes.

Try This!

* **At mealtimes, explain how you are dividing up food.** "We have eight spring rolls for the three of us. Let's each have two, and then see who's still hungry."

* **Engage children in deciding how to share.** "How can we divide three buns among the four of us? What if one bun is larger than the others?"

* **When children are playing, ask how they are sharing.** "What's the fairest way to share these blocks? How did you decide to divide up the stickers?"

* **Discuss with children:** "Is sharing equally always the same as sharing fairly? Does everyone always want the exact same amount? Does everyone need the exact same amount?"

As children decide how to share, encourage them to explain their thinking. Although they may not yet use the words *division* and *fraction*, they are learning about those concepts!

— **Angela Chan Turrou**
Senior Researcher and Teacher Educator,
UCLA Graduate School of Education

Visit www.charlesbridge.com/storytellingmath for more activities.

To my editor, Alyssa, for trusting me with this story; to Marlene, Molly, and Theresa for brainstorming math concepts; and to my Aunt Ruth, whose love of dim sum inspired the setting—N.Y.

For my little angel, Yujin—V.K.

This book is supported in part by TERC under a grant from the Heising-Simons Foundation.

At the time of publication, all URLs printed in this book were accurate and active. Charlesbridge, TERC, the author, and the illustrator are not responsible for the content or accessibility of any website.

Developed in conjunction with TERC
2067 Massachusetts Avenue
Cambridge, MA 02140
(617) 873-9600
www.terc.edu

Published by Charlesbridge
9 Galen Street
Watertown, MA 02472
(617) 926-0329
www.charlesbridge.com

Printed in China
(hc) 10 9 8 7 6 5 4 3 2 1
(sc) 10 9 8 7 6 5 4 3 2 1

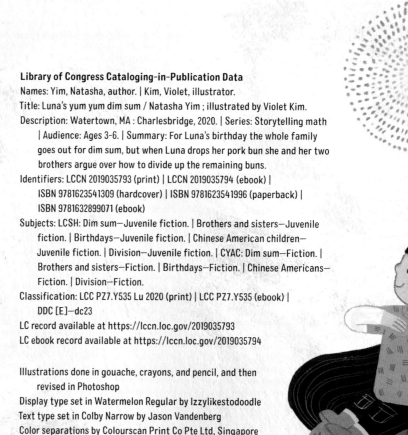

Library of Congress Cataloging-in-Publication Data
Names: Yim, Natasha, author. | Kim, Violet, illustrator.
Title: Luna's yum yum dim sum / Natasha Yim ; illustrated by Violet Kim.
Description: Watertown, MA : Charlesbridge, 2020. | Series: Storytelling math | Audience: Ages 3-6. | Summary: For Luna's birthday the whole family goes out for dim sum, but when Luna drops her pork bun she and her two brothers argue over how to divide up the remaining buns.
Identifiers: LCCN 2019035793 (print) | LCCN 2019035794 (ebook) | ISBN 9781623541309 (hardcover) | ISBN 9781623541996 (paperback) | ISBN 9781632899071 (ebook)
Subjects: LCSH: Dim sum—Juvenile fiction. | Brothers and sisters—Juvenile fiction. | Birthdays—Juvenile fiction. | Chinese American children—Juvenile fiction. | Division—Juvenile fiction. | CYAC: Dim sum—Fiction. | Brothers and sisters—Fiction. | Birthdays—Fiction. | Chinese Americans—Fiction. | Division—Fiction.
Classification: LCC PZ7.Y535 Lu 2020 (print) | LCC PZ7.Y535 (ebook) | DDC [E]—dc23
LC record available at https://lccn.loc.gov/2019035793
LC ebook record available at https://lccn.loc.gov/2019035794

Illustrations done in gouache, crayons, and pencil, and then revised in Photoshop
Display type set in Watermelon Regular by Izzylikestodoodle
Text type set in Colby Narrow by Jason Vandenberg
Color separations by Colourscan Print Co Pte Ltd, Singapore
Printed by 1010 Printing International Limited in Huizhou, Guangdong, China
Production supervision by Brian G. Walker
Designed by Jon Simeon and Sarah Richards Taylor